THE BEST MARIACHI IN THE WORLD

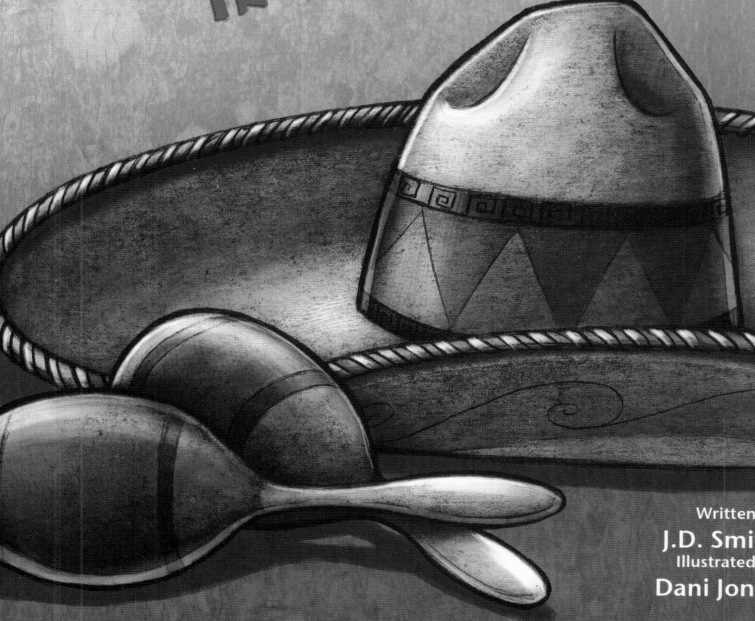

Written by
J.D. Smith
Illustrated by
Dani Jones

For all the Gustavos of the world,
and for one very special Magaly. — JDS

For Nik and Shan. — DJ

Smith, J.D.

The Best Mariachi in the World / written by J.D. Smith; illustrated
by Dani Jones; translated by Eida de la Vega – 1 ed. – McHenry, IL ;
Raven Tree Press, 2008.

p.:cm.

English Edition
ISBN 978-1887744-99-7 hardcover
ISBN 978-1887744-98-0 paperback

Bilingual Edition
ISBN 978-09770906-1-7 hardcover
ISBN 978-09794462-4-5 paperback

Spanish Edition
ISBN 978-1887744-97-3 hardcover
ISBN 978-1887744-96-6 paperback

SUMMARY: Gustavo wants to be in the family mariachi band,
but he cannot play the violin, trumpet or guitar. He
finds his place in the band with his singing talent.

Audience: Pre–K to 3rd grade.
Available as an English–only format, Spanish–only format, and Bilingual,
with mostly English story and concept words in Spanish.

1. Ethnic Hispanic & Latino—Juvenile fiction. 2. Bilingual books.
3. Picture books for children. 4. Spanish language materials—Bilingual.
I. Illus. Dani Jones. II. Title. III. El mejor mariachi del mundo.

Library of Congress Control Number 2008920929

JBS042018

THE BEST MARIACHI IN THE WORLD

Written by J.D. Smith
Illustrated by Dani Jones

Raven Tree Press
A Division of Delta Systems Co., Inc.
www.raventreepress.com

Gustavo was the worst mariachi in the world. Everyone else in the family band could play an instrument. But not Gustavo. He did not play songs at weddings or at restaurants. He did not wear a charro suit or a sombrero.

Sometimes he reached for the bow of his brother Raymundo's violin. Raymundo quietly said, "Don't touch the bow of my violin. You might break it. It is not for you."

Sometimes Gustavo tried to play his Uncle Enrique's brass trumpet. Uncle Enrique gently said, "Put down my trumpet. You might drop it. It is not for you."

Gustavo did not even try to pick up his father's guitar. It was taller than he was.

Gustavo wondered how it would feel to strum the long strings. He imagined everyone would listen. People would look at him. The men and women would get up and dance. All the children would dance and clap.

He would be Gustavo, the great mariachi.

But that would never happen. No one would let him play. He would always be the worst mariachi in the world.

Even his cousins would not let him try to play their guitar, trumpet or violin.

They would say, "This is not for you."

"Hmm," Gustavo thought, "I want to be in the band—in the mariachi band. But what can I do?"

Gustavo got up one
morning before dawn.
He looked out into the
desert and saw the cacti.
The saguaro cactus stood
like huge trees. The nopales cactus lay close
to the ground. The sky was a black bowl of
stars. Somewhere an owl hooted.
A coyote padded over
the sand. Everything
was beautiful.

No one was there to play.
But he had to stand up
and sing. He just had
to sing.

He sang softly at first, barely moving his lips.

The next day he got up a little earlier. He sang in a whisper.

The day after that Gustavo, sang a little bit louder.

The following day he sang louder still. He did not think about where he was or how early it was.

Before the first rooster crowed, before the first light of day peeked out from the east, Gustavo sang, and sang at the top of his voice.

One by one, the lights in the houses came on.

A man called out, "What is happening?"

A woman wondered, "Who is that?"

A child asked, "Who is that singing?"

Gustavo kept singing.

He sang of traveling men. He sang of faraway places and of coming home again.

He sang all the songs he knew. He sang all the songs that he knew like his own name.

A crowd of people came out to listen.

At last Gustavo finished singing. He was done with his songs. He turned to go inside. It was time to feed the chickens.

The people started to clap. They liked his singing! They were clapping for his songs.

"Gustavo!" they called out. "Bravo! Very good!"

They kept clapping. Women waved their handkerchiefs.

His brother gave him a big hug and said, "You are a real mariachi."

His father said, "You, my son, just may be the best mariachi in the world."

His cousins carried Gustavo, the best mariachi, into the house. They made him a huge breakfast. Then they fed the chickens for him.

The next time the band played, Gustavo wore a charro suit. He wore a sombrero. He sang the songs that had brought everyone outside.

All the people clapped and cheered. He took off his sombrero and took a deep bow.

"This," Gustavo thought, "is for me."

It is estimated that Mariachis have been playing their own style of music since about 1880.

No one knows exactly how they got their name. Some people believe that they are named after a kind of tree whose wood was used to make stages or the musical instruments that mariachis play. Those instruments include the Spanish guitar (guitarra), the guitarrón, a small bass guitar with a rounded back, the vihuela, a high–pitched guitar with five strings, and violins. Most mariachi bands also have at least two trumpets.

Besides their instruments, mariachis are known for their unique clothing, the traje de charro (cowboy suit). This outfit consists of a close–fitting jacket and pants with brightly colored trim, and a wide sombrero with bright embroidery. At first only men wore the traje de charro and played mariachi, but in the last fifty years more and more women have joined them, either in mixed or all–woman bands.